To Kate

Love Nonna & Pa
2020

Author Amy Cohlmia Greco
Illustrator Goran Vitanovic

ISBN: 978-1-7344488-1-8

For copyright permission, book readings, and other inquiries, please
email the author at notsousualpress@gmail.com

This book is dedicated
to my friends, family, and Molly
who have all inspired me
along the way

Along the Way with Molly

by Amy Greco

illustrated by
Goran Vitanovic

Are you ready, Molly?!
MOLLY

Molly was more than ready to play!

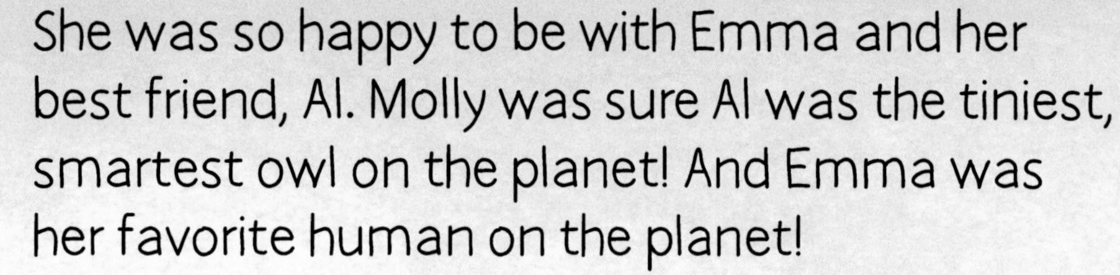

She was so happy to be with Emma and her best friend, Al. Molly was sure Al was the tiniest, smartest owl on the planet! And Emma was her favorite human on the planet!

It was only a few weeks ago that Emma found Molly at the local shelter. It was love at first sight.

Emma knew they would be best buddies. She showed Molly her new home, and they were both very happy.

Emma tossed the bone. It flew higher and farther...farther and higher. It looked like it would travel forever!

Molly was excited to chase after her bone...
it was like running to find treasure.

Molly ran after the bone. Along the way, she saw children sliding down the slide.

Molly patiently waited her turn and slid happily down the slide. She enjoyed playing with the children and realized the fun was worth the wait.

After sliding several times, she again ran after
the bone. She ran so fast Al could barely hang on!
Along the way, they saw ants working.
Molly wanted to stop and watch them.

They are so tiny!
And they are mighty! Ants can lift many times their body weight. Now, let's go get that bone!
Molly

Molly DID rush toward the bone,
but along the way, she splashed in a mud puddle.

Molly

Al flew to his favorite fur buddy after he shook the yuck off his feathers.

He found Molly near a patch of colorful flowers she stopped to smell along the way. Bees buzzing around the flowers had Molly's eye... and nose!

Molly thought the bees sure looked busy. She also remembered SHE better get busy finding that bone!

Along the way, she just HAD to stop to watch a mama duck and her ducklings. Molly thought the baby ducks were so cute!

Al watched his friend splash and play in the pond.

Suddenly, Molly jumped out of the pond. She was having so much fun, she almost forgot about the bone! Molly thought Emma would be worried if she didn't get her the bone soon.

Emma loved Molly, but she wasn't worried.

She was watching her pup the whole time.

Molly finally spotted her bone near a flowery bush. Al was happy... and relieved as well. Finding the bone with his friend was fun and exhausting all at the same time!

Molly was super excited to find her bone. It really was like finding treasure! She also learned something very important that day…

She learned that the BEST treasures were the friends she met, things she learned, and fun she had **along the way**!

Bee Facts with Al

Bees help other plants grow.

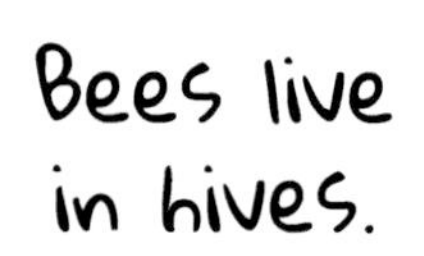

Each bee hive has a queen bee.

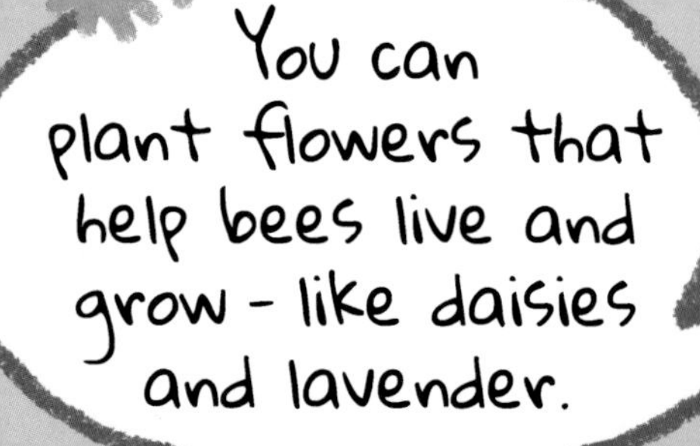

Thank you
for helping other
readers find us by
leaving us an
amazon review!

Made in the USA
Coppell, TX
01 December 2020